MOUSE'S
Christmas
WISH

MOUSE'S
CHRISTMAS
W I S H
A PICTURE CORGI
BOOK 978 0 552 57469 3
First published in
Great Britain by Picture Corgi,
an imprint of Random
House Children's Books
A Random House Group Company
This edition published 2011
3 5 7 9 10 8 6 4

Picture Corgi Books are
published by Random House Children's Books,
61-63 Uxbridge Road, London W5 5SA
www.**kidsatrandomhouse**.co.uk
www.**randomhouse**.co.uk
Addresses for companies within The Random House Group
Limited can be found at: www.randomhouse.co.uk/offices.htm
THE RANDOM HOUSE GROUP Limited Reg. No. 954009
A CIP catalogue
record for this
book is available
from the British
Library. Printed and
bound in China.

Mouse's Christmas Wish

Judi Abbot

PICTURE CORGI

to Nico and Veri,
with love and fun!

It was very nearly Christmas and Rabbit
was sending invitations to all her friends.
'One each for Duck and Bear, Dog and Mole
and, of course, one for Mouse.'

The next morning, in a little house deep in the forest, an invitation arrived, and it said:

'Hurray!' shouted Mouse. 'That's just how I wished I'd be spending Christmas. Now, I've got so much to do before I can set off on the journey to Rabbit's house.'

On the furthest edge of the lake, Bear had also received an invitation.
'Whoopee!' he yelled. 'I'm on my way!'
He hurriedly threw some things into a bag and set off.

High up on the top of the big snowy hill, another invitation had arrived. 'Ah-ha,' smiled Dog. 'Now I can try out my new sledge.'

Over on the other side of the lake, Duck was already very busy. 'I need to bake a cake, a pudding, pies, tarts and sweets... I can't wait to spend Christmas at Rabbit's house!'

And down at the railway station, standing on the platform, Mole was already waiting for his train. 'How nice,' he said. 'I shall enjoy spending Christmas with my friends.'

Meanwhile, Mouse had started packing.
'I'll need clothes for cold weather and warm, and for rain and snow.
And I'll take towels and sheets, some blankets, pans and plates,
extra shoes, hats and scarves...'

But the suitcase popped open. It just wouldn't stay shut.
'Oh no,' squealed Mouse. 'How am I going to carry it all?'

Bear had set out across the lake.
He loved to skate and he was
very good at it.

'What a pleasant journey,' thought Mole
as he gazed out of the train window.

By now all the others had arrived
at Rabbit's house.
'Ah, here you are!' she beamed.
'Now Christmas can really begin.'

Meanwhile, Mouse had dug
himself out of the snow. But it was dark
and he was cold and wet.

'It's impossible,' he sobbed. 'I just can't go on.
It's too far, it's too late. And all I wished for was
to spend Christmas with my friends.'
Slowly he trudged home, back
through the snow.

His friends were having a wonderful time. They hung up the decorations, placed the presents under the tree and put all the tasty treats out on plates.

'But where is Mouse?' asked Rabbit.
'Wherever can he have got to?'

Mouse had gone to bed.

'My Christmas wish will
never come true now.'
His tears fell as he pulled the
covers over his head.

Just then there was a ring at the door.

'Oh dear, oh dear, who can that be?' Mouse sniffed. 'It's too late for the postman and it's not early enough for the milkman.'

'SURPRISE!' everyone yelled.
'Come on, Mouse, you're late. We've come
to take you to Rabbit's house for Christmas.'

And they walked
to the end of
the lane,

past the old
fir tree,

round the
corner,

and there was
Rabbit's house.

'Whatever took you so long?' asked Mole.
'You practically live on Rabbit's doorstep!'

'Now we can really start enjoying Christmas,' said Rabbit. And everyone agreed. They sang songs, played games, ate treats and told stories.

'Ahem,' said Mouse. 'My dear friends, I thought my Christmas wish would never come true. Thank you for making this the best Christmas ever.'

Later that night, Mouse was woken by a magical sound. Shooting across the sky was the one final visitor everyone wishes to see at Christmas.

Happy Christmas, Mouse!

MARGRET & H.A. REY'S

Curious George Feeds the Animals

Illustrated in the style of H. A. Rey by Vipah Interactive

Houghton Mifflin Company Boston

Based on the character of Curious George®, created by Margret and H. A. Rey.
Illustrated by Vipah Interactive, Wellesley, Massachusetts: C. Becker, D. Fakkel, M. Jensen, S. SanGiacomo, C. Witte, C. Yu.

The text of this book is set in 17-pt. Adobe Garamond.
The illustrations are watercolor and charcoal pencil, reproduced in full color.

Library of Congress Cataloging-in-Publication Data

Curious George feeds the animals / based on the original character by Margret and H. A. Rey.
p. cm.
Summary: Curious George gets in trouble by feeding the animals at the zoo, but when a parrot escapes from the rainforest exhibit he is able to save the day.
RNF ISBN 0-395-91904-5 PAP ISBN 0-395-91910-X PABRD ISBN 0-395-92340-9
[1. Monkeys—Fiction. 2. Zoos—Fiction. 3. Parrots—Fiction.] I. Rey, Margret, 1906–1996. II. Rey, H. A. (Hans Augusto), 1898–1977. III. Vipah Interactive.
PZ7.C921364 1998
[Fic]—dc21

98-21327
CIP AC

Printed in Singapore
TWP 20 19 18 17 16 15

This is George.

George was a good little monkey and always very curious.

One day George went to the zoo with his friend, the man with the yellow hat. A new rain forest exhibit was opening and they wanted to be the first ones inside.

But when they got to the new exhibit, the doors were closed. "We'll have to come back later, George," the man said. "Why don't we visit the other animals while we wait?"

First they stopped to watch a zookeeper feed the seals. When he tossed little fish in the air, the seals jumped up to catch them. Then they barked for more.

It looked like fun to feed the animals!

"Would you like something to eat, too, George?" asked the man with the yellow hat, and he bought a snack for them to share.

When they stopped to see the crocodile, George remembered how the zookeeper had fed fish to the seals. He was curious. Would the crocodile like something to eat?

George tossed him a treat — and the crocodile snapped it out of the air!

Next they visited the koalas. George thought the koalas were cute. Here was a friendly one—she was curious, too. She wanted to see what George was eating, so he held out his hand to share.

George shared his treats with an elephant

and a baby kangaroo.

George was making lots
of new friends at the zoo.
The lion was already eating, but
the hippopotamus tried a snack.
Next he gave a treat to an ostrich.

COLATE

Then George saw the giraffes.
What fun to feed a giraffe!
Giraffes usually have their heads up high in the trees, but George could see these giraffes would be easy to feed.

But as soon as he held out his hand, a zookeeper came running. The zookeeper looked angry. Was he angry with George? George didn't know — and he didn't want to stay to find out. He slipped away . . .

and the giraffes were happy to help!

But where did George go?

He was trying his best to hide. But little monkeys can't stay still for long. When George wiggled, the zookeeper was waiting. "I see you!" he said.

Just then another zookeeper hurried by. "Come quick!" she yelled. "Someone saw the parrot!"

The first zookeeper led George to a bench.

"The parrot from our new exhibit escaped and I must help find it," he explained.

He told George to wait for him there, and before he left he said, "Don't you know you're not supposed to feed the animals? The wrong food might make them sick."

George felt awful.

He didn't know he wasn't supposed to feed the animals. He didn't want to make them sick.

George was looking at the treat in his hand when all of a sudden,

a big bird swooped
down and snatched it right up!
Now George knew he wasn't supposed to
feed the animals . . . but this one had helped itself.

A zookeeper passing by was happy to see George. “You found the parrot!” she said. “We’ve been looking for this bird all day.”

When she saw George’s snack, she said, “This isn’t the best thing to feed a parrot, but a little won’t hurt. Would you like to help me put him back where he belongs?”

George was glad to help after all the trouble he had caused, and together they went back to the exhibit.

"There's our problem," the zookeeper said, pointing to a hole in the netting. As the zookeepers discussed how to fix it, George had an idea. . . .

He climbed up like only a monkey can, and when he reached the hole—he tied the netting back together!

Meanwhile, the first zookeeper returned. "Catch that naughty monkey!" he yelled. "He was feeding the animals!"

"But that little monkey found the parrot," another zookeeper told him. "And look—he fixed the netting. Now we can open the exhibit."

When George came down, all the zookeepers cheered.

Finally the celebration began and the doors were opened. The man with the yellow hat was there, and he and George got to be the first ones inside!

As George walked in, the zookeepers thanked him for all his help. "Please visit anytime!" they said.

George couldn't wait to come back and see his friends. But next time he'd remember, unless you're a zookeeper…

RAIN FOREST

DON'T FEED
THE
ANIMALS!